Me and My Dad

First published in 2009
by Wayland

This paperback edition published in 2010 by Wayland

Text copyright © Amanda Rainger 2009
Illustration copyright © Simone Abel 2009

Wayland
338 Euston Road
London NW1 3BH

Wayland Australia
Level 17/207 Kent Street
Sydney, NSW 2000

Series Editor: Louise John
Cover design: Paul Cherrill
Design: D.R.ink
Consultant: Shirley Bickler

A CIP catalogue record for this book is available from the British Library.

ISBN 9780750258098 (hbk)
ISBN 9780750260237 (hbk)

Printed in China

Wayland is a division of Hachette Children's Books,
an Hachette UK Company

www.hachette.co.uk

Me and My Dad

Written by Amanda Rainger
Illustrated by Simone Abel

WAYLAND

On Saturday my Dad comes.
He calls for me at eight.

I can't wait to see my Dad.
I hope he won't be late.

5

Dad took me to the funfair, and I went on lots of rides.

6

The Ghost Train was really scary, but I loved the bumpy slides.

He took me to the cake shop, and I ate a sticky bun.

I got jam down my jumper.
Dad said, "Oh dear, son!"

Dad took me to the seaside.
We went there on the train.

We swam and paddled in the sea, but it began to rain!

When it was my birthday,
Dad took me to the zoo.

14

We saw the giraffes
and elephants.
I liked the monkeys too.

Last week we went fishing.
I had a little net.

I nearly got a fish but
I fell in and got wet.

If it isn't raining,
we play football in the park.

I kick the ball into the net,
until it gets too dark.

I think I like it best of all when Dad takes me to the pool.

We splash and have
a lot of fun.
My dad is really cool!

When Dad takes me home again, I always feel so sad.

START READING is a series of highly enjoyable books for beginner readers. **The books have been carefully graded to match the Book Bands widely used in schools.** This enables readers to be sure they choose books that match their own reading ability.

Look out for the Band colour on the book in our Start Reading logo.

The Bands are:

Pink Band 1A & 1B

Red Band 2

Yellow Band 3

Blue Band 4

Green Band 5

Orange Band 6

Turquoise Band 7

Purple Band 8

Gold Band 9

START READING books can be read independently or shared with an adult. They promote the enjoyment of reading through satisfying stories supported by fun illustrations.

Amanda Rainger writes books and TV programmes for children learning French and Spanish. Best of all, she likes making up songs and stories — especially in rhyme! She works in a shed in the garden, with a tortoise, a fox and a chaffinch for company.

Simone Abel has illustrated over 200 books for children and has even won some awards. Best of all, she likes drawing people and animals, although she has just finished illustrating a book about cakes, which was great fun! She lives in Yorkshire, with her husband who is a painter, and their two daughters.